MW00424492

THE SPOKES

THE SPOKES

Miranda Mellis

SOLID OBJECTS

NEW YORK

IT'S MY DELIGHT
Words and Music by Renford Cogle, Brent Dowe and Trevor McNaughton
Copyright (c) 1970 Universal – Polygram International Publishing, Inc.
Copyright Renewed
All Rights Reserved Used by Permission
Reprinted by Permission of Hal Leonard Corporation

LOVER'S HOLIDAY
Written by Edward Thomas, Clifton Thomas and Bob McRee
Used by permission of Bro 'N Sis Music, Inc. on behalf of Crazy Cajun Music

ISBN-13: 978-0-9844142-4-6
ISBN-10: 0-9844142-4-X

SOLID OBJECTS
P.O. Box 296
New York, NY 10113

THE SPOKES

When I set out on this trip, I planned to come back. It's true that when I embarked, the return date of my trip was not set, but I had not imagined this ... duration. If that is what it is. I remember the high, winding, narrow roads along the coast, the vertigo.

And I remember at the ferry building there were a series of warnings, one of which was about the peculiar sort of "jet lag" one sustains in a realm whose primary substance is not time. The customs agent had recited, and required me to repeat after her, line by line, a litany of warnings about the nature of my destination. The only thing I remember now is the first warning: *Do not eat the food*, which I did, of course, within the first "day" (though that unit of time becomes meaningless without a sun).

I picked up my bag and boots after running the security gauntlet. As I turned to put on my boots, I tripped on the lip of a plastic mat. A uniformed young woman wearing latex gloves caught me as I toppled forward, and steadied me. She gripped my arm longer than was strictly necessary. She looked at me intently, with clear gray eyes. "Be careful, ma'am," she said. "Watch your step. Do you have a copy of the ferry schedule?" I did not. She turned around and pulled a small folded schedule from a stack behind her. She pressed it into my hand and firmly advised me not to lose it.

I laced up my black boots on a long wooden bench. There were several musicians emerging together from the line and collecting their instruments. A musician next to me opened a case and examined his trumpet. He put his mouthpiece on and blew. Then he put his trumpet together and played a familiar tune, the Melodians' "It's My Delight": *I love you, I love you, I really do.*

I walked slowly, listening to him play as I made my way down a ramp, a long hallway, and a flight of stairs. I came to the dock, a wobbling ramp of looped planks, and boarded the great rusty ferry, which was splattered with bird shit and tied off with ropes. I found a seat on the deck where long benches faced the diminishing shore. I fell asleep in my seat as the boat wended its way across the black river, over which lay a gray tule fog.

I dreamed I was in a bathtub. I had left the faucets on and the room was flooding. My mother, Silver, came in and rebuked me. She threw green towels on the floor and sopped up the water. We'll have to take these to the laundry, she said, they'd never dry in here. The floor became an ocean, the bathtub our boat. We were cold. We wrapped the towels around ourselves. We rode the waves but the tub was sinking. My mother bailed out the water with her hands, her hair gathered and scooped back. I looked around for a rescue ship as we sank. Then I looked down and saw my station wagon loping down into the heavy water.

I woke cold, unable to see, hear, or sense anything, not even my own weight. I had kicked over my purse, and some of its contents were beneath the bench. I bent over to collect them. A few pieces of paper, including the ferry schedule, fluttered away. I stood to chase after them when I saw a light, and then many more lights. I observed the crowd as we approached the shore. They flickered into view like so many lanterns. Three dogs ran back and forth along the quay. When I stepped off the boat, one trotted over, licking my hand and wagging his tail. The other two raised their heads and smiled. A lone child in a tilted orange hat with a rooster feather debarked behind me. The dogs ignored the child and the child ignored the dogs. The child talked instead to her hands, or should I say with her hands, which she was using as two puppets.

I petted the dog, who grinned amiably. The other dogs walked slowly back to the wall. One stretched, seeming to bow in my direction; he circled several times and then lay down a little heavily, as if something weighed on him. He nosed around himself chaotically, his dirty mane sticking out. Catching my eye, he glanced down the quay suggestively. I followed his gaze, and with a little shock I made out my mother. She looked just as I had last seen her, the day of her fall from the high wire. She wore her tight faux-emerald-and-ruby-studded tunic over a sheer dark-blue bodysuit, long, sharp macaw feathers in her bound hair. Glitter sparkled on her purple opalescent lips, and her eyes—one eyelid silver, the other gold—glistened brightly. Her short cape and slippers were sequined. For so long it seemed as if the gap between us would only grow. Now suddenly we were three feet apart.

Silver greeted me in the typically polyphonic voice of the dead, like the eager, chaotic valence of a tuning orchestra. Like crying, and a drill, and a xylophone, a chorus of one. "You must be hungry?" she said. I was dizzy with joy and nervousness as I went toward her, but she was looking past me. Who was she talking to? I turned around to see, behind me, the child: a much younger version of myself. Now I remembered the hat . . . I'd worn it constantly for months after my first unhappy haircut. I'd had hair down to my waist. My mother took me to the yo-yo man, a geometer who had good scissors. When he was finished, my hair was the same length all the way around, a yo-yo–like sphere.

Clearly my mother did not see me, though I was standing right in front of her. Instead she saw this other, younger me. I spoke, I gestured. Neither of them made me out. I looked around. Was I the only invisible one here? Everyone seemed to be enjoying his or her reunions. My mother caressed my younger self's face, squatting down to gather her child into her arms. They walked hand in hand down the platform to a kiosk. My mother bought my younger self a tin of cold green gelatin, which she ate hungrily. I followed them I knew not where, my mother in her Spokes Cirque Rêve costume, as colorful as a summer bird, and my younger self in the slyly cocked orange hat.

It was not the first time in my life that I was invisible in a public place, if one can say of the afterworld that it is public. (Perhaps there is nowhere more public.) As a child I learned to blend in with the other spectators. I did not perform, though I longed to; my parents had other hopes for me. But the person I had grown into was not someone my mother knew anything about; perhaps that was the reason she could not see me as I was, but only as I had been. Unlike some, she had not spent her afterlife keeping current, i.e., haunting. She never returned the calls I made to her in my sleep. She never responded to the letters I wrote her on desperate days. She had her own death to live. In life too, she'd never talked much. When she was not rehearsing or performing, she was distracted and melancholy. On stage she smiled fervently, as if to smile was to bless. Offstage she was secretive, closemouthed.

I gather some families talk about everything (though all individuals have their reservoirs of silence). I only knew Silver was the last performer in the Spokes line, grew up in the same caravan that her ancestors had traveled in, performed the same tricks in the same towns and villages, and knew, just as her foremothers had known, that she risked the void every time she entered the ring. My father, Leo, was twice her age and an epileptic. "If nature had taken her course, I would have gone first," he had said. But gravity is nature.

It started to thunder in the distance: A storm approached, but no rain fell. The trumpet player passed me, walking

8

slowly, playing Peggy Scott's "Lover's Holiday": *Maybe we can slip away.* I greeted him but he looked right through me. He was the only passenger I recognized. With my first pang of worry, I turned and watched him walking away. I wondered if I should follow, if he was on his way to catch a ferry home. But if time is not the substance of this universe, I thought, how could we know when it was "time" to return? I felt as if I could stay a thousand years or twenty minutes and it would make no difference. In any case, I had lost the ferry schedule.

I glanced around the station as I followed my mother and my younger self. I told myself to pay close attention to the path we were on, so that I could find my way back. I had never felt so disoriented; no sun, no East. At the end of the street, at the first right turn that my mother, myself, and I took, there was, hanging above the door of a very different kind of station farther down, Philip Guston's *The Tormentors.* I paused to look at the volcanic tongues of red paint. I told myself, when you see that again, you'll know you're on your way back. "What's that place?" my younger self asked, pointing. "The Tormentors, that's their station," my mother said, "in the Sinister Quarter."

The people at that station were gray, black, and white. Other than the painting, nothing at that station had any color. Light, absorbed or reflected by a surface, normally fractures and becomes color. It was as if the painting had absorbed all the available light, with none left over for the people or the pocked, rusted station.

We passed another station, Lautrec's *At the Moulin Rouge*. Was this my mother's stop? There was the trumpeter, standing just outside with all of the other musicians who had been on the ferry with me. They played exuberantly and comfortably, like old friends. A small crowd gathered and danced, including my mother and my younger self. They were a closed circuit, from which I was excluded. Why this should be the case I did not know. Was my invisibility the result of something I had failed to do? I had yet to learn the laws of recognition here, which are not moral in the same way they are at home, where dreaming is neither a virtue nor a skill (as it has proved to be here).

The crowd was not held by the music. Apparently the dead were incapable of paying attention to anything for very long. A few wandered toward a station with a fogged-in Malevich hanging overhead.

My mother and younger self sat on a bench and watched the dead mill around. I stood behind them and listened in on their conversation. "Where are they all going?"

my younger self asked my mother. "Nowhere," said my mother. "But they look so busy, like they are going somewhere," my younger self said. "Well," Mother said, "they feel they should be." "But where are they supposed to be?" my younger self asked. "Nowhere in particular," Mother replied. "Why don't we tell them?" my younger self said. "You can try," my mother said. My younger self called out to the crowd, "Hey! Stop! Where are you going? You're dead— there's nowhere to go! Hey!" One shade stopped and asked, "Yes?" My younger self said, "Where are you going?" "I can't remember, but I must go on," he said. "Why do you think you have to go on?" she asked. But he was gone.

Where do I think I'm going? I said aloud. But of course, they weren't aware of me. I walked around to the bench where my mother and younger self were talking. I stretched out next to them and fell asleep. For the second time on this trip, I dreamed. In the dream there was a giant baby with a head like a white stone, big dark eyes like galaxies, and smooth infant skin. She stood slowly on her toddling legs, her arms outstretched, and when she stepped forward she caused an earthquake. The dream state we were in shook apart from the mainland into the sea. There was a narrow, connecting bridge of earth left. We humans walked it, migrating to the center of the continent to forge a new society based on non-duality.

in her dream

When I awoke I was sore from sleeping on the bench. To my astonishment my mother and my younger self were looking right at me. They spoke to me about my dream, which they called a movie, for dreams in the afterworld are movies for the dead.

My dream movies had made me visible, and yet they still did not know who I was. "I doubt there could be a society based on non-duality," my mother said, "but I really enjoyed the cinematography." My younger self said, "Yeah, in your movie, even though California fell into the sea, when all the people walked together to the center of the world to make a new society, I felt happy." I wanted to take credit for the dream, but it was none of my doing; I didn't even remember it that well. The only thing that mattered was that though they didn't recognize me, at least my mother and younger self now saw me. (It seems life can change you so much you wouldn't know yourself.) "Your smile is familiar," my mother mused. "You remind me of someone." I was just going to tell them who it was when she said abruptly, "Let's go now," and turned away.

We ascended a spiral stairwell at the center of the station. We came to the roof of the station where tables and chairs and waiters and eaters were scattered all around. Some people sat on the ground singing. Others sat on the ledge of the roof with their legs dangling down, nervously looking around. A wall, the inside façade of the station, played films: the dreams of the living, a constant festival for the dead.

The musicians from the ferry played accompaniment. So much music. Mother explained that music gives the dead patience, "the highest virtue." A waitress came with dainty bowls of green gelatin, which I found both satisfying and delicious. I partook, forgetting the warnings against eating the food. As I ate, my younger self began to flicker in and out of view. With a jolt and a flat, echoing sound like an enormous lid closing, she vanished. My mother cried out and held my head in her hands, pressing her forehead against mine. In eating the food I had inadvertently closed off the passage back; now she knew me.

Surroundings can change a person. I have been living at our station, *La famille de saltimbanques*, in the Happy Quarter, in an apartment with extremely long hallways and large rooms, with my mother, for a while (I really couldn't say how long). Perhaps it is the endless length of the hallways, the height of the ceilings, the lack of sun (and therefore day and night), or the simplicity of our thixotropic meals (gelatin, our food; melted gelatin, our drink), but I have a nagging feeling that I have forgotten something.

I have just discovered that there are gods who live among the dead. I saw one for the first time yesterday, very well dressed. I was leaning out the window, elbows on the sill, looking at the Francis Bacon Head station when he walked out of it. I didn't know he was a god at first, I didn't know what he was, but I definitely knew he was not a shade.

His aura was assured, brittle, and bright, his jaw large, and his teeth sharp. A confused shade asked the god politely if he had any idea what she was supposed to be doing. The god looked at her as if at an abstraction and went on. The shade called after him, "Where am I supposed to be?" I called, "Why does it matter?" She looked up at me, surprised, and asked, "How can I continue this way without knowing?" I said, "Why do you think you need to continue this way?" She walked off, shaking her head.

Whereas the dead were preoccupied with trying to remember something (mostly where they were supposed to be and what they were supposed to do once they got there), there was an air of self-assurance in the god's aspect: He was where he was. Though the shades were lost, still, they comprehended their realm better than the gods, according to my mother, whose own father had been a god. "Would you say that the gods are alienated?" I asked. "No," she said, "because they don't know that they don't know. In order to know this world, you must be able to die. They can't die, so they can't know this world." "What if a god wants to know it?" "Like I said," she said, "you have to be

Silvers dad = god

able to die." "How does a god die?" "By eating the apple," she said. She held up one of several tarnished brass apples that sat on our mantel. I learned to juggle with them. I used to play-eat them as a toddler, informally preparing for gnosis and death. She tossed several at me. I caught them and tossed them right back; we volleyed. "What was it like having a god for a parent?" I asked. "It was awful," she said. "He was so critical." "What was your mother like?" "She was a saint." "She was very kind?" "She was a statue."

I still don't understand why my mother lingers here among the arrogant gods and lost souls, of which she is neither. Until now, she has always been evasive on the subject. Sometimes she answers my questions with questions. Usually she won't even answer my questions, or talk to me at all, though lately she's become more voluble. "Why do gods bother to come here?" I asked her. "Sometimes they have projects to do," she explained. "Mostly they're couriers. Also, of course, this is an interesting place for them." "Is that why you stay?" "I stay because I'm waiting for my message," she said. I was surprised. I pointed out that it was usually the living who came to the land of the dead seeking a message. "That's true in mythology," she said, "but in reality, the living come to take the place of the dead." "What is the message?" I asked. "If I knew," she said, "would we still be here? I only know it's a kind of ticket. It takes you to the place you need to be, and it tells you what to do once you get there. It's what everybody is waiting for."

At that moment I remembered the dream I'd had on the ferry. How she had bailed out water as our vessel sank. How long we tried to swim, drifting apart. How it felt to lose sight of her, to sink.

My mother would wait as long as she had to; there was nothing to do but wait. When I first arrived—shall I say "long ago"?—she thought I had the message she was waiting for.

She wanted to know how my siblings were. I couldn't tell her much. After her fall everyone had scattered, and I was younger by ten years than my nearest sister. Life had quickened for all the members of the family, and we sped along, doing our best to keep pace, but in one arena of the family's past, where our lives would always overlap in memory, life did not quicken, rather it remained absolutely still, as if not to be seen.

The statement *What we cannot speak about we must pass over in silence* had proven useful to us. For if a subject won't yield any understanding, then what is to be done? A family naturally gives up on the insoluble, the unanswerable, the hopeless cases—they are like fossils or mythology. Even if they involve local events within common memory, such subjects are practically Paleolithic in their random (lonely, common, exilic) indecipherability. Though perhaps "subject" is not the right word for this part of no speech, an unpredicated, empty space.

Families are experts on such rifts—between event and memory, between all sides of the story, the living and the dead, childhood and everything else. For the Spokes, the subject of our silence formed an unacknowledged nucleus around which we orbited with backs turned, looking out at the universe, sometimes sideways at one another, but never inward. If history brings us all together, secrets dwell on the underside of it, beyond the remedy, reach, and solvency of speech.

Call family secrets species of silence, except they are mineral, not biological but calcified.

I imagine a skull buried under a mountain, or a box with a rusted lock at the bottom of a pit.

The right accounting might break the lock, for perhaps that which can be honestly reckoned with can change—

that is, whereof one can speak, one updates the subject; things can look different in the light—those things that we can talk about are subjects subject to change: They change under discussion.

But as with fairy tales, myths, political campaigns, and legends, what if it mattered more who spoke and when than what they said? Isn't it more important to be believed than to speak the truth? Haven't we learned from politics and circus barking that speech is not for truth, but rather for manipulating perception? Or haven't we learned from placebo effects and folktales and art that if only specific people, or substances, give the sought-after effect, it doesn't necessarily follow that this is because they are what they seem to be, but only that their seeming to be overcomes our doubt?

so true!

As so many villains and clowns have discovered, it is not enough, or even necessary, to say the true words.

The book, the charm, the dagger, the amulet, the enchanted animal, the weather, the genie, the god, the witch, the princess, the dragon, and the frog that are unleashed/ revealed/conjured/transformed/disenchanted/animated/ deactivated or released by magic words require that the right person speak them at the right time. The season, the hour, the garb, the stars, and the record must be in order for the magic to work. Sometimes the impossible is the missing ingredient.

If my mother was waiting for a message, for my part, I had a question. I kept forgetting it, though; I forgot for ages. And when I remembered I had a question, it was another age before I remembered what it was. It was like reaching for something but not having long enough arms. I reminded myself: Next time you remember your question, ask it right away. That is how it is around here: You have to remind yourself to remember.

And finally I did remember. And I did ask. At first she equivocated: "'Why?' is not a spiritual question, Lucia." "I don't care," I said.

"It wasn't a hard trick." "The Möbius strip? It's not exactly easy," she laughed. She put her arm around my shoulder. I waited. "Why wash those bones?" she asked. "What's done is done." "It's not done," I insisted, "or why would I be here?" We sat in the latest of her long silences.

I saw it all again, vividly, a welter of images like overlapping nightmares, the crowd in the round, her liquid dexterity as though drawn in the air by mercury, glinting in the shins, you couldn't keep track of her limbs, and then, absurdly, the beam of waltzing light that was her solo, as if she was slapped out of the air, reddening on the black Marley floor. I have stared my whole life at that image, captioned: *It isn't what you think.*

The grief never diminishes. It's just gradually obviated by the persistence of the present tense, the quivering copula between disasters. How are things moving and yet so static? I wondered, involuntarily witnessing for the thousandth time in my mind's eye her reverse flight.

Suddenly Silver spoke, saying, "Imagine walking all together on a dock over the ocean on a foggy day. We come to the end of the pier, and everyone turns to go back. But I seem to perceive that it continues; the air clears and I see a bridge ahead. I'm curious, so I keep walking. Eventually I find myself here. But for those left behind, I simply fall off; I am gone. And I was gone, for them. Two different realities, coexisting more than theoretically." Something

she leaves her family because she sees this bridge / saw an opportunity thudded through me, thick, fibrous, and dusty, an old animal running from the answer I didn't want: that it had not been a fall, but a capitulation. *surrender → suicide*

She seemed to backpedal. "It was an accident and an expression of purpose." But those aren't the same at all, I *seems to be on purpose* thought; she's confused. Is it possible that even she doesn't know what happened? "That makes no sense," I said cautiously. "I know," she said, "it wasn't what I thought." "What wasn't?" "The future—it wasn't ahead of me." "You're making no sense," I said. "So you've already said. But that is a good way of putting it," she said. "I lost my human sense, and that is the only way of knowing for you."

But what way of knowing could there be for a human, other than the human way of knowing? Even in this so-called "afterworld," didn't I remain human?

"Were you that unhappy?" I asked. She said, "Life seemed unreal; a death-dream. In any case, it wasn't choice, but chance.... We don't possess our selves, you know." *chance / choice*

"What was the moment of death like?" I asked. "It's very quick," she said, "like an exhale. I remember the chaotic vertigo and the feeling that at last: It was done. How much simpler life would be, now that I was dead. No more feeling or feeding, hunger or rage. And no more patriarchy—no more of that five-thousand-year-old boulevard of crime." "Did you even wonder how the rest of us would feel?" "I thought death would be complete non-identity: Who would there be to recriminate? But I was wrong—for though the drama of the body had ended, the drama of consciousness was by no means over."

She was not expressing remorse, exactly, though something had shifted. Not just between us, but all around us. She did not even possess herself, or so she said: How could she have been mine then, to lose? Or, could one belong more to others than to one's self?

Who, what was I mourning? How to describe that loss? She was one thousand birds in migration; tired light; warmth, depression, and curiosity. She was real emptiness. But so am I.

"What was it like in between life and death?" I asked. "It wasn't really like anything," she said. "But even like has to be like something," I said. She thought it over and said, "Then it was like the back of the head seeing the back of the head in Magritte's mirror, or the earthen body traces of Ana Mendieta, or Godard's faceless conversationalists. I was bodiless, yet looking at something looking. Though it isn't quite right to say 'looking' or even 'I': I became a fiction. Or at least 'I' seemed to be only a barely extant device with which to see myself not seeing myself. Where was my mind? I can't say. And I'm not talking about that cabbage of pleated irrigators in our head, that network of custard and lightning, the brain. You know the joke about looking for a black cat in a dark room in which it is not? It was most like that. Though if I didn't exactly see her, I could still hear the cat—I mean I couldn't locate the mind, but I could echolocate it."

Silver is a duelist

There was a knock on the door. My mother went to answer it and in strode the god I had seen earlier—bright brittle big jaw. He gave her a notice informing her that she had mail waiting for her at Nancy Spero's *Tongues*—the message station in the Liminal Quarter—and he left.

We went to Spero's *Tongues* to pick up my mother's mail. In the enormous station there were people singing all along curving balconies, throwing confetti and blowing bubbles. Nowhere did I see the burning wheels, pumping tortures, frozen faces, despairing devils we primitives are taught to expect. Perhaps if I went to the Tormentors I would see them, supplicants of futility and shame. But if this is not hell, if it's heaven, where are the candles, dresses, white fire, harps, Maxfield Parrish clouds, love-addled angels? In heaven I imagined feathers, so many feathers, everyone drinking coppery nectar in the bright light, geniuses standing by windows combing each other's hair, snow on the statues, and long-bearded beauties with piercing eyes, charismatic manners, happily contradicting each other, swimming over abysses with imperturbable nerves.

But this afterlife imaginary is arbitrary. The dead look painted. Periwinkle walls or sea green, golden frames and ancient, perfect faces, wandering characters, blind psychics, folds and folds of heavy cloth, spontaneous singing at the post office. They dance, watch dream movies, eat gelatin. So what do they think about? The living can't help but think terrible things; do the dead? Or do they have control over their thoughts? If I found my relatives from, say, a hundred years ago, what would they discuss? Pogroms? Communism? Piroshkis, books? Do the dead read? I suddenly realized I had not been this clearheaded in ... It had been so long, I had forgotten irony.

And by the way, apparently the dead do have a hard time reading. Silver's hands shook with excitement as she opened her message. She squinted and ran her pointer finger under the sentences like a child, but she couldn't make them out. "I recognize this language," she said anxiously, "and I see the letters, but I don't know what they mean." "Let me see," I said. I could read it easily. It said:

Tell your living to remember *Silver's message!*

Push yourself into the mountain until you explode into the sun

The moment I finished reading it, we were transported to the apartment of my father, Leo. He was lying in bed with his eyes open. He couldn't see us or hear us. "We have to try to get him to understand," my mother said. I leaned over and touched him and suddenly I was inside him.

Underneath his sternum and all the way up his throat we felt a hard snap, the whip of old red fear: a fit. We closed our eyes and put a long, frail hand over them, trembling. We grimaced. Suddenly our torso, arms, and legs vibrated violently, our eyes widened, and our tongue lolled out. We shook like a frightened dog. But in five minutes the seizure passed.

We slept. We dreamed we were searching on a map spread out on a table. We found a small town called Silver and tried to find the road from here to there. Then I took control of our hand. I held a pen as best I could. It was hard to work his hand, the pen—I could barely write anything at all. I managed to scrawl just one word on the map: *Remember*. To our amazement he said, "Don't worry, I will." What a relief; he understood!

L eo drove and drove—the cemetery was so far away, it was in the middle of nowhere. It's a good place to be, he thought, if you have no body—the middle of nowhere. Now where does that expression come from? He wondered. Nowhere has no circumference, so how can it have a middle? That's the point of it, he answered himself, that's the joke: There is no middle of nowhere. So to say something is in the middle of nowhere is just to say it is as far away as possible, in every direction, from somewhere.

It was hot and the car had no AC. He was sweating profusely by the time he arrived. The cemetery was enormous, the biggest one he knew, the size of a town, practically. Usually you'd go to the office to get a map to find your dead, but the office was closed. It was the middle of the day in the middle of the week: Why closed? He suddenly remembered that on the train yesterday he had been way-laid by a Lubavitcher. "Are you Jewish?" the man had asked with a smile, holding pamphlets in his left hand and a new-born baby in his right. The infant faced downward, his tiny torso cupped in the man's hand. "No," Leo lied, annoyed. "Oh," the man said with a friendly smile. "The reason I ask is that there is a holiday tomorrow, Shavuot." "I don't do that," Leo had said brusquely, turning away.

He felt humiliated, embarrassed. If he had listened to the fanatic, given him some credence, he would have known the cemetery would be closed! He had come all this way, in such heat. Why couldn't he have brought the old map? Why didn't he know his way around by now? The truth was he had gotten out of the habit of coming a long time ago. Still, he sort of thought he would or at least should know where Silver was, but then he'd never come without Lucia, "the human compass." She could find anything, navigate anywhere. Had they stayed at the circus that would have been her act, reenacting scenes of losing and finding.

He, on the other hand ... he felt like he should give up. But rather than leave, he found himself wandering. The graves were in rows, lined up, all facing one direction. And then he'd turn a corner and find hundreds of graves lined up in rows facing the other direction. In fact the graves faced all directions, section by section. He wandered, searching, in vain. At last he found a bench and sat under a sycamore in the middle of this nowhere. It was quiet and a breeze blew through the trees. Gradually he became aware, as though he could remember through his feet, that there were thousands of human bones underneath him, side by side in the dirt of the graveyard, gridded like a city, orderly and decaying.

The weather changed; the air was cooling and white mist skidded over the hill in front of him. The clouds, loose and thin, seemed purposeful, as if to show him what the air was doing, or that they meant something by their movements.

I have taken the plates off the broken wagon and am walking down a coastal highway. I feel free—no longer in search of my ghost. I'm lighthearted as I walk and think. About the dead, for example, their habits, their blind spots, and their obfuscations. They are humbler than the living, but no less confused. They remind me of people recently released on their own recognizance after a prolonged period of institutionalization, in which bureaucrats are in charge, where threats and universal schedules subtend every bodily need or experience. The Cartesian dead, I'd call them.

I remember I asked Silver to take me to the beach but she said there were no oceans. "Where do vacations happen then?" I asked. She replied, as she often did, at an angle: "The grayer and more dusty the life, the more need for

Disneyland." "Is there a Disneyland here?" I asked. "No," she said. "Why would there be? There's no need for Disneyland if no one has to work." But it seemed to me that people were working. At least they appeared to be on their way to and from work, wearing coats, carrying satchels, looking straight ahead, leaning forward as if to get ahead of themselves. Silver said that wasn't the case. It was just the way the dead walked that made it seem so. "The amnesiac hustle," she called it.

I wondered why they were all so similar. Death looked no different from life, with even less justification. They didn't have to pay rent or buy commodities, so why did they continue to look around nervously for the boss? Did they think they were on vacation, that it was the weekend? The bulk of them would stand in bunches under an old, faded sign, "Job's Creation," waiting for something, though my mother said the Redemptive Quarter had shut down long ago.

Silver explained that our afterworld was populated by the recently deceased, who seemed trained not so much to act as to get somewhere—wherever—"on time." Music calmed them, art gave them places to go, but neither music nor art helped them think about where they were. The songs and pictures that surrounded us were like markers, descriptions of the past, while the present was unreal. That the present should be unreal would make sense if you were marking time in prison, where it would be only reasonable to look to the future. But after life? To wait, even in death, for the starting gun?

"What are the ancient dead like, then, the pre-capitalist, the pre-clock-time, the pre-imperial dead?" I asked. But Silver didn't know. "Perhaps they are invisible to us, out of time, unrepresentable." I wondered how they would comport themselves, if the afterworld would be more recognizable to them, or if at least they would be more comfortable in deciding for themselves what time it was, what actions to take, how to mythologize the universe. But Silver warned me against romanticizing older shades. "We've been this kind of human, anatomically speaking, for two hundred thousand years," she said. "If we don't know ourselves, how can we know the ancestors?" Still, I suggested, we should try.

ACKNOWLEDGMENTS

Versions of *The Spokes* have appeared in *Vertebrae* and *Conjunctions*—many thanks to those journals' editors, Richard Chiem and Bradford Morrow. "What we cannot speak about we must pass over in silence" is Ludwig Wittgenstein's seventh proposition from the *Tractatus*. "Even like has to be like something" is from the poem "Luster" by Rae Armantrout. "The grayer and more dusty the life, the more need for Disneyland" is paraphrased from Guy Debord. This story gratefully samples dreams, Roman mythology, the Book of Genesis, circuses, Philip Guston, Nancy Spero, Kazimir Malevich, Pablo Picasso, Francis Bacon, Henri de Toulouse-Lautrec, Ana Mendieta, Jean-Luc Godard, René Magritte, the Melodians, Peggy Scott, and Aleksandr Sokurov's *Russian Ark*. Heartfelt thanks to Eirik Steinhoff for editorial feedback.

I want to learn more and more to see as beautiful what is necessary in things; then I shall be one of those who make things beautiful. Amor fati: let that be my love henceforth!

—Friedrich Nietzsche

MIRANDA MELLIS is the author of *None of This Is Real, Materialisms,* and *The Revisionist. The Revisionist* was a finalist for The Believer 2007 Book Award and has been translated into Italian, Croatian, and Polish. Mellis is a founding editor at the Encyclopedia Project. She lives in San Francisco.